Japanese
Boys' Festival

by Janet Riehecky
illustrated by Krystyna Stasiak

created by Wing Park Publishers

ℙ CHILDRENS PRESS®
CHICAGO

Library of Congress Cataloging-in-Publication Data

Riehecky, Janet, 1953-
    Japanese Boys' Festival / by Janet Riehecky ; illustrated by
Krystyna Stasiak ; created by Wing Park Publishers.
        p.   cm. — (Circle the year with holidays)
        ISBN 0-516-00695-9
        1. Festivals—United States—Juvenile literature.   2. Japanese
Americans—Social life and customs—Juvenile literature.   3. United
States—Social life and customs—Juvenile literature.
[1. Festivals—United States.   2. Japanese Americans—Social life
and customs.]   I. Stasiak, Krystyna, ill.   II. Title.   III. Series.
GT4803.A2R54   1994
394.2′62′0952—dc20   93-47639
                                                                                    CIP
                                                                                     AC

Japanese
Boys' Festival

"Mom!" Kenji shouted. "Come outside.
There are great big fish flying in our front yard!"
Kenji raced out the door to get a closer look.

A tall bamboo pole stood in the front yard.
It had two paper fish attached to it. Wind blew

in through the mouths of the fish. The fish
swelled out so they looked real. They wriggled
back and forth as if swimming in the air.

Kenji's mother and father and his little
brother, Hiroshi, followed him outside.

"Those are carp," Kenji's father said. "Carp are strong and brave. They can swim against the current and even fight their way up a waterfall."

"I remember," said Kenji. "Today is May 5th, Boys' Festival and Kite Day!"

"That's right," said Kenji's mother. "The top fish is for you, Kenji, and the bottom one is

for you, Hiroshi. We put up the carp to honor
our sons and to encourage them to be brave
and strong like the carp."

"Why is Kenji's fish bigger than mine?"
Hiroshi asked.

"Because he's older," their father explained.
"Come inside," he added, "and see what else
we have."

On some special shelves in the living room, Kenji's mother and father had put swords, spears, and figures of warriors.

"Wow!" said Kenji, as he admired the miniature armor. "These are great."

"Can I play with them?" asked Hiroshi.

Kenji rolled his eyes. His mother explained, "Hiroshi, these aren't playthings. These are special keepsakes to remind us of important values like courage and strength."

"Now, hurry and get ready," said Kenji's father. "There's a festival at the community center."

Lots of people were already at the community center when Kenji and his family arrived. There were many booths with games to play and places to buy souvenirs. Kenji bought a

plastic sword and pretended to be a samurai
warrior.

"Hey, Kenji," his friends called out when
they saw him. "Let's have a battle."

Kenji and his friends pretended to fight fiercely.

"Can I play too?" Hiroshi asked.

"Why do you always want to tag along after me?" Kenji said with a scowl, but he let Hiroshi join them.

Kenji played for a while with his friends.
"Someday I will have lots of adventures like
these," he said to Hiroshi.

Kenji and Hiroshi passed a booth selling food, and Kenji bought some sweet rice cakes wrapped in oak leaves. He gave one to Hiroshi.

"Mmm. This is good," Hiroshi said as he took a big bite. But at that moment, he dropped

the rest of the cake on the ground. Hiroshi
started to cry.

Kenji rolled his eyes in frustration, but he
said, "Don't cry, Hiroshi." Then he bought him
another cake.

Soon it was time for the best part of the day—the kite flying contest!

Lots of people were gathered in the baseball field next to the community center. Kenji and Hiroshi tried to find a spot where they could

see. But some bigger boys pushed in front of them. One of them bumped into Hiroshi, knocking him to the ground.

"Help me!" Hiroshi cried. It looked as if he might be stepped on by the crowd.

"Don't worry, Hiroshi," Kenji exclaimed. "I'm here." Kenji hurried to Hiroshi and helped his little brother stand up. Then he put his arm around his shoulders.

One by one the contestants sailed their kites into the sky. Kenji's father had a kite that looked like a hawk. The breeze was just strong enough for an exciting contest. Each kite-flyer tried to tangle his kite string with the others. Each one

pulled and tugged and twisted, trying to make the other kites lose their balance and fall to the ground. The last kite in the sky would be the winner.

Kenji and Hiroshi laughed and cheered. They watched their father zigzag his kite around and bring down a dragon kite, then zigzag again, avoiding someone else. Soon his hawk and a large green carp were the only kites in the sky.

Carefully Kenji's father measured out a little extra string. Then with a twist and a turn he swung his kite around. The last two kites tangled, and the green carp lost its balance and fell to the ground. Kenji's father had won!

"I can't wait until I'm old enough to be in the contest," Kenji said, watching his father with admiration. "I want to be just like Dad."

"I could be in it too," said Hiroshi.

Kenji smiled at his brother. "Someday we'll both be in it," he said.

At home that night, Kenji's mother prepared special baths for each of her sons. After the dirt was washed away, Kenji and Hiroshi soaked in a tub with clean, warm water. Their mother put the long, sword-like leaves of the Iris plant in the water. This was to give the boys strength.

"I will grow up to be strong and brave," Kenji said to his mother, as she tucked him in that night.

"From what Hiroshi told me, you already are strong and brave," said his mother. "You

let him play with you and your friends, bought
him an extra rice cake, and protected him from
the crowd. I'm very proud of you, my son."
And Kenji's mother kissed him goodnight and
turned out the light.

Making a Carp

(Teacher will need to help.)

Carp streamers are a traditional display on Boys' Festival. Here's one way to make them. You will need: a round metal ring about three or four inches in diameter; a long sheet of paper, such as newsprint; paints; tape; string.

1. Cut a sheet of paper about one foot wide and two feet long.

2. Roll the paper into a tube with the same diameter as the metal ring. The edges should overlap slightly. Cut away any extra.

3. After you've cut the paper to fit the ring, flatten the paper again and paint a carp on it. (You may prefer to use crayons or markers.) Use the pictures of carp in this book.

4. After the paint has dried, roll the paper carp back into the tube shape and tape the edges. Place the metal ring in the carp's mouth and fasten it in place with tape.

5. Tape a piece of string to the top inside of the carp's mouth and hang it where the wind can blow through it. Carp streamers are traditionally displayed on bamboo poles.

2 ft.

1 ft.

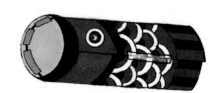

Rice Cakes

The traditional rice cake for Japanese Boys' Festival is called *Kashiwamochi*. It is a round, flat cake filled with sweet bean paste. You may be able to buy them in a Japanese grocery store, but if you can't, you can still enjoy rice cakes.

Buy rice cakes at a health food store or regular grocery store. Ask members of your class to bring in different toppings. You may try peanut butter, different flavors of jelly, marshmallow creme, caramel, banana slices, or anything else that sounds good to you. See who can come up with the tastiest combination!

Making Kites

You may also wish to make small kites to decorate your classroom. Simply cut a diamond shape out of construction paper and decorate as you wish. You may have some fun adding elaborate or funny tails to your kites.

Japanese Girls' Festival — Dolls' Day

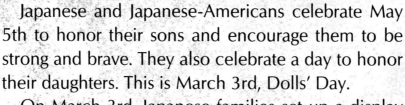

Japanese and Japanese-Americans celebrate May 5th to honor their sons and encourage them to be strong and brave. They also celebrate a day to honor their daughters. This is March 3rd, Dolls' Day.

On March 3rd, Japanese families set up a display of beautiful dolls in their homes. Special shelves are set up. There can be three, five, or seven shelves, but the top shelf always contains the prince and the princess dolls, each beautifully dressed. On the shelves below there will be three ladies of honor and five court musicians. Some families add noblemen, servants, guards, and footmen. Other things, such as furniture, playing cards, fans, and musical instruments are also added. Every detail is carefully studied, because these dolls are not to be played with; they are to be looked at and admired. Many of the dolls will have been in the family for generations.

The most important event of the day is a miniature feast. The daughter or daughters in the family will prepare tiny dishes of soup, fish, vegetables, rice cakes, and other special foods. Some of the food is placed on tiny plates in front of the dolls — who are given tiny chopsticks. Tea is also served.

On this special day each Japanese girl feels as if she is the princess on the top shelf of the display. But the girls also look forward to Dolls' Day for one other reason — it's the one day of the year that their brothers have to behave!

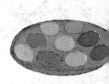